Finn~

# Billy Miller

# MAKES A WISH

Love and
Wishes!.
Grammie
and

Papa

# Billy Miller
## MAKES A WISH

## Kevin Henkes

Greenwillow Books

*An Imprint of* HarperCollins*Publishers*

Billy Miller Makes a Wish

Copyright © 2021 by Kevin Henkes

First published in hardcover by Greenwillow Books in 2021;

first paperback publication, 2022.

The text of this book is set in 13-point Century Schoolbook BT.

This book is printed on acid-free paper.

Book design by Kevin Henkes

Hand-lettered display type by Ryan O'Rourke

Library of Congress Cataloging-in-Publication Data

Names: Henkes, Kevin, author, illustrator.
Title: Billy Miller makes a wish / by Kevin Henkes.
Description: First edition. |
New York : Greenwillow Books, an imprint of HarperCollins Publishers, [2021] |
Companion to: The year of Billy Miller. | Audience: Ages 8-12. | Audience: Grades 2-3. |
Summary: "On his eighth birthday, Billy Miller wishes for something exciting to happen. None of his wishes are answered the way he expects, but he does have lots of surprises—and the final one is possibly the best one ever"—Provided by publisher
Identifiers: LCCN 2020050744 | ISBN 9780063042797 (hardcover) | ISBN 9780063042810 (ebook) | ISBN 9780063042803 (pbk ed.)
Subjects: CYAC: Wishes—Fiction. | Birthdays—Fiction. | Surprise—Fiction. |
Family life—Wisconsin—Fiction. | Wisconsin—Fiction. | Humorous stories.
Classification: LCC PZ7.H389 Bil 2021 | DDC [Fic] —dc23
LC record available at https://lccn.loc.gov/2020050744

First paperback edition

22 23 24 25 26 PC/LSCH 10 9 8 7 6 5 4 3 2 1

 Greenwillow Books

*For Laura, Will, and Clara—my every wish come true*

# 1

When Billy Miller blew out the eight candles on his birthday cake, he made a wish. He wished that something exciting would happen.

Not more than ten minutes later—even before the present opening had begun—a police car and an ambulance flew past Billy's house and raced down the block. The wail of sirens stopped nearby.

Without thinking, Billy ran out the door,

turned in the direction of the flashing red lights, and followed after them.

"Wait up," his father called.

Along the block, bats swooped from the trees and fireflies pulsed in slow motion, but Billy didn't notice. He just ran. Neither a police car nor an ambulance had ever come to Maxwell Street before. At least, not that Billy knew of.

The police car and the ambulance had parked in front of Mr. Tooley's house at the far corner.

Billy stood, still as glass, at the edge of Mr. Tooley's driveway. His father caught up to him and firmly placed his hands on Billy's shoulders.

"What's happening?" Billy whispered into the green darkness.

"I don't know," said Papa. "I don't know."

Billy was mesmerized. He watched Mr. Tooley's house intently. It dawned on him that being a paramedic when he grew up might be a good idea. It would be better than being a regular doctor because you'd still get to help people, but you'd also be able to drive fast *and* use a siren.

Neighbors were gathering on the sidewalk and driveway in clusters. Papa slipped away and talked to a couple people, then came back to Billy.

After lingering a few more minutes, Papa said, "I think we should go home. Mom and Sal are waiting. We still have birthday business to attend to. And I still have some packing to do."

"Papa? I mean, Dad," said Billy. "Do you think Mr. Tooley's okay?"

"I hope so."

Lately Billy had been trying to call his father "Dad," rather than "Papa," which is what he'd called him for as long as he could remember. It was a hard habit to break. And even when Billy remembered to call him Dad, he still *thought* of him as Papa. Maybe he always would. He was having the same problem calling Mama "Mom."

In the silence that followed, the stars seemed to draw closer, as if they, too, wanted to know what was going on.

"Let's go," said Papa. He directed Billy toward home and gave him a gentle shove. They walked quietly across Mr. Tooley's perfect lawn.

It was strange. It was as if the excitement Billy had felt about his birthday had been shut off inside him and a different excitement—because of the police car and ambulance—had been stirred up and had taken over. There was another feeling that was jumbled with it, becoming stronger. It was a certain uneasiness because Papa was going on a trip tomorrow. He was going to an art camp for adults. He'd be gone for four nights. Billy wished he could go with Papa.

Billy turned back for one last look at

Mr. Tooley's house. The paramedics were taking a stretcher out the front door. There definitely was someone on the stretcher.

Is this happening because of my wish? Billy wondered.

Papa saw the stretcher, too. But he kept guiding Billy forward. "Homeward, buddy," he said in a jolly voice. "I could use another piece of cake."

They continued home. Now Billy noticed the fireflies. How could he not? They were flickering like Christmas lights. Blink, blink, blink. Blinking as if to say, "Why?" "Why?" "Why?" Why did I make that wish? thought Billy.

Billy forgot about Mr. Tooley as soon as he walked through his own front door.

"Where'd you go?" asked Billy's little sister, Sally, whom everyone called Sal. "It's your *birthday*!"

"If you hadn't come back soon, Sal would have opened your presents," said Mama.

"It's *my* birthday soon," said Sal. She would be four in a month. She was more than ready.

Billy saw his parents share a few serious words—quickly and quietly. Papa shrugged and Mama nodded and then everyone piled onto the couch with Billy's presents.

"Open mine first!" said Sal. "It's really good. You'll like it." Beaming, she thrust a package at her brother. "I wrapped it myself," she said proudly.

"I can tell," said Billy.

"Mama helped," Sal explained. "She tied the bow."

The present looked like a big ball of crumpled tissue paper of many colors held together with quantities of tape. It was tied nicely with red ribbon.

Billy untied the bow and tore into the

wrapping. "There's nothing here," he said. "Is this a joke?"

"Keep going," said Sal, giggling.

Finally, when he was nearly ready to give up, Billy uncovered a little blue eraser in the shape of an elephant. Its trunk was missing. He didn't know what to say.

"It's from my collection," said Sal. "But I didn't want it anymore. I lost its nose. So now you can have it."

"Thanks a lot," said Billy. He rolled his eyes. But he wasn't disappointed or too annoyed, because he knew he had real presents from his parents.

"Now I'm mostly just keeping my little

whales, so maybe you could have some of my other eraser animals, too," said Sal. "Maybe I'll give you some for Christmas."

Billy scanned his presents, deciding which to open next.

"Wait," said Sal. "I'll be right back. I forgot the Drip Sisters. The girls should be here." She flew out of the room.

"She's something," said Papa. He often said this.

"I can't believe the Drop Sisters are out of our lives," said Mama. "Replaced by the *Drip* Sisters."

"At least the Drip Sisters are more portable," said Papa.

"But easier to lose," said Mama. She raised her eyebrows and thinned her lips, making a funny face. "I can see it now. . . . "

The Drop Sisters had been Sal's obsession and constant companions. They were five identical yellow plush whales named Raindrop, Dewdrop, Snowdrop, Gumdrop, and Lemondrop. Sal used to take them everywhere, which was a problem at times. She'd cart them around in a grungy pillowcase. She still slept with them, but they stayed on her bed for the most part.

The *Drip* Sisters were little erasers shaped like whales. Sal had five of them as well, also yellow, named Raindrip, Dewdrip, Snowdrip, Gumdrip, and Lemondrip.

Lately, when Billy was mad at Sal, he'd say she was the biggest drip of all.

"We're back!" said Sal, reentering the living room. Her eyes were sharp, bright as sparks. "The girls are right here," she said, patting her bulging pocket.

"Then let's get this birthday show rolling," said Papa.

Joyfully, Billy ripped into his other presents. They were definitely better than the trunkless elephant eraser.

Billy got a new soccer ball. It came with a pump and a needle that looked like a sleek silver insect that you inserted into the ball to add more air.

He got a T-shirt with a bat printed on it,

which he put on instantly. It fit perfectly—it was roomy, so it didn't pinch at his armpits the way some of his shirts did.

The bat was cartoony with goggle eyes. It had big sharp teeth and claws. And the shirt smelled new. Billy repeatedly pulled the shirt up, buried his face in it, and inhaled deeply.

He got a chapter book, a graphic novel, and a blank book in which he could write or draw whatever he wanted to.

He also got a deluxe set of markers—fifty in all. The markers were in a cardboard box made to resemble wood. The box said *Premier* in fancy letters. It was impressive.

There were several kinds of markers in the box—double-ended, brush tipped, chisel tipped, fine pointed, extra-fine pointed. There were fat markers and one super-duper, especially fat marker.

And the colors! There were markers of every color Billy knew and some with names he'd never heard of before: magenta, crimson. Some of the names he needed help pronouncing: cyan, chartreuse. Looking at the box of markers with their different-colored caps made Billy think of a box of candy.

Obviously Sal was thinking something similar, because she was drawn to the markers as if by a magnet. First her eyes and then her fingers were all over them.

"Hey," said Billy, squinting at Sal. "They're mine." He pulled the box closer to his lap and protected it with his arms. "It's *my* birthday."

The crumpled look on Sal's face softened Billy. "Do you want all my bows and ribbons?" he asked. He hoped this would be a good diversion, distract Sal from his markers.

"Yes!" Sal chirped. "Happy birthday to me," she sang as she gathered the bows and ribbons and draped them over her shoulders and around her neck. She pranced around the living room.

Billy scooted off the couch and made a nice pile of his presents. He counted the markers to make sure there were, in fact, fifty of them.

Mama and Papa stayed on the couch. Papa had his arm around Mama. They whispered back and forth and then they kissed. Once, twice, three times.

Billy groaned and turned his head away. It was funny—he pretended that seeing his parents be all lovey-dovey with each other made him uncomfortable. But, actually, he liked it when he saw his parents show affection. It made him feel safe.

Sal settled down. Now she was wrapping her plastic headband with the ribbons and bows. When she had the headband completely covered, she put it on, pushing her dark, curly hair away from her face. She looked like she was poking her head through a festive, lumpy wreath, making her round face seem even more round.

"When you blew out your candles, what did you wish?" Sal asked Billy.

"Can't tell," said Billy.

"It's not fair," said Sal. "You get eight wishes and I'll only get four on my birthday."

Billy jerked around to look at his parents. "Is that true?" he asked. "Do you get a wish for every year? I thought it was just *one* wish."

"That's what I've always thought," said Mama. "One wish. I've never heard about more wishes. If it's true, it's news to me."

"It sounds like a good idea," said Papa, smiling. "Think how many wishes *I'd* get."

Billy's mind was racing. Maybe he could make seven more wishes. Maybe he could undo his wish that made the ambulance come. Maybe he could wish that Mr. Tooley lived to be one hundred.

"Do you think birthday wishes come true?" asked Billy.

Papa shrugged.

"Sometimes yes," said Mama. "And sometimes no, I suppose."

That's not very helpful, thought Billy. "What if you make a wish and then you think it was a bad wish?" he asked. "Can you have a redo?"

No one answered Billy's questions, which were drowned out by a new song from Sal.

But Papa came toward Billy and tapped him gently on his head. "Let's get that new soccer ball of yours and break it in."

"Now?" asked Billy. It was late. It was dark.

"Why not?" said Papa. "It's your birthday."

It was very dark. The air was warm and damp and smelled of summer. Papa flipped the switch by the side door and a blurry-edged curve of light filled the backyard.

Billy smelled his soccer ball the way he'd smelled his shirt. It, too, smelled new. And it looked new—the white parts were so white. And it felt new—smooth and shiny and polished.

"Kick it to me," said Papa.

Billy did. The ball even felt new to Billy's foot, if that's possible.

"Nice," said Papa.

They passed the ball back and forth. Papa moved the ball from one foot to the other like a professional.

"You're really good, Dad," said Billy.

"Thank you," said Papa. "I don't think I'm as good as you think I am."

Billy tried to dribble the way Papa did.

After a few more kicks, Papa asked, "Is something bothering you?"

"Nope," said Billy.

"Are you sure?"

Billy nodded. He couldn't think what to say.

"Well, if you decide that something is bothering you, you know you should tell me or Mama."

"I know."

Thankfully, Papa changed the subject. "I can't believe you're eight," he said. "And a third grader."

"Well," said Billy, "technically, I'm a second-and-a-half grader. I'm not in third yet."

Papa laughed.

It was June. School had just ended. Billy did *not* want to think about third grade. He wanted summer to last forever.

The ball sailed between them. Papa could do a few tricks with the ball, but what amazed Billy most was how accurately Papa could aim the ball. Sometimes it was hard for Billy to get the ball to go exactly where he wanted it to go. Not for Papa.

All of a sudden, Papa stopped the ball with his foot. He rolled it onto his toes and balanced it. Then he flipped the ball upward, caught it, and tossed it to Billy. "You know," said Papa, walking toward Billy, "if you need another wish, I think you should take it."

Silence.

"And," Papa continued, "to make it official— just hold up your finger, pretend it's a candle, and blow it out as you make your wish."

"Would that work?" asked Billy.

"It's worth a try," said Papa.

As they entered the house, Billy slipped

his soccer ball into Papa's arms. "I'll be right back," said Billy.

Billy turned off the outside light and returned to the yard. With the light off, the yard was black. Blacker than before. It was so black, it seemed that the yard could go on for miles or that it could end in a few feet.

Billy raised his index finger. He rose up on his toes. He whispered, "I wish that Mr. Tooley is okay." Then he drew in a deep breath and blew at his imaginary candle.

Billy wandered in circles repeating the wish six times in his head before he went from the darkness outside into the golden light of the kitchen.

# 4

"Can I use your markers?"

Billy opened his eyes to slits and Sal was right there. They were nose to nose. He could feel her breath on his face.

"What?" he said, his voice froggy, his eyes gluey with sleep.

"Can I use your markers?" Sal repeated. "Please?" Slatted sunlight striped her face. "I need to make a symphony card."

"What's that?" Billy asked. He had never

heard of a symphony card.

"Well, I'm not sure," said Sal. "But Mama's doing one, too. It's because Mr. Tooley died."

Billy lifted his head, leaving a wet patch on his pillow. "He did?"

"Yep."

"Are you sure?"

"Uh-huh. Can I use your markers?"

Billy blinked and sat up, wondering if he'd been dreaming. His bedroom was washed in pale light so that the edges of the walls and furniture were soft. He could tell it was early, but Sal was already dressed, set for the day. She hopped onto her brother's bed and sighed. "Markers?" she said, her eyes pleading.

Fully awake, Billy threw off his thin

covers and ran to the kitchen to look for Mama.

Mama was sitting at the kitchen table, talking on the telephone in a hushed voice. There was an opened note card in front of her; she'd been writing on it. Billy leaned in toward her and mouthed the word: *Mom?* Mama held up her index finger to say: *Wait. I'll be right with you.*

But Billy didn't want to wait, so he looked for Papa.

Papa was in the driveway, loading the car for his trip to art camp.

Billy had temporarily forgotten about art camp. And now, he was fully aware of the thought of it—the reality of it—and a funny feeling ran down his back. But first things first.

"Papa—*Dad*—did Mr. Tooley die?" asked Billy.

Papa pulled his head out of the back of the car and slammed the door. He tugged at his curly orange beard. "He did," said Papa.

"Really?"

Papa nodded. "It's sad, but he lived a long time. He was ninety-two."

"Do you think he died yesterday night when we were eating my cake?"

"I don't know."

"Do you think he was okay and then he just died suddenly on my birthday?"

Papa tugged on his beard again. "I don't

know much about it. But Mama talked to Mr. Tooley's daughter this morning. She said he'd been sick for a while. So he hadn't been okay."

Billy needed to be certain. "So he *hadn't* been okay?"

"That's right."

"So, if it wasn't my birthday, he would have died anyway?" asked Billy.

Papa inclined his head. He sighed a big, thoughtful sigh. "Mr. Tooley dying has nothing to do with your birthday," he said. And he said it in the voice that always made Billy feel better, the voice that made Billy think that Papa was the smartest man in the world.

Instantly, Billy was relieved. When Sal

had told him that Mr. Tooley had died, Billy thought that it was his fault because of the wish he'd made. The world—including himself—had seemed to shift and unravel, to dissolve into a million pieces. And, now, just like that, everything had come back into place, into focus. Billy felt steady again. Solid. He felt like a normal eight-year-old boy.

# 5

Papa was gone. That simple fact changed the way the house felt. The air seemed thicker somehow to Billy. Thankfully, Mama was home.

Mama worked during the school year. She was a high school English teacher, so she had the summers off. Papa was an artist who worked at home. He made sculptures and assemblages out of found materials. The garage was his studio. Usually he was the one who was always there, and so when he wasn't, the difference was real.

Mama, Billy, and Sal were at the kitchen table.

"What do you think Papa will make at art camp?" asked Sal.

"I don't know," said Mama. "But I'm sure it will be wonderful."

"My symphony card is wonderful," said Sal.

"It's *sympathy*," said Billy.

"That's right," said Mama. "Sympathy."

"What is it again?" asked Sal. "What's it for?"

"Well . . . ," said Mama, tapping her pen on the tabletop. Obviously, she was thinking, choosing her words carefully. "It means that we understand that Mr. Tooley's family is sad and we share that feeling." She stopped tapping. "And we tell them."

"Mine is just pictures," said Sal. "Flowers."  She pursed her lips, tilted her head, and looked at her drawing. "It's nice," she said. Mama glanced at Sal's work. "Very nice."

"My flowers will cheer them up," said Sal.

"Careful with my markers," Billy warned. "Don't press too hard."

Billy had felt so relieved when Papa had spoken to him about Mr. Tooley that he let Sal use his markers. But he wanted to keep an eye on her. He wanted to make sure she didn't ruin them. Or take any of them.

Also, before Papa drove away, he looked right at Billy through the half-lowered car window and said, "Help Mama with Sal." His eyes were loving but piercing. Then he winked.

Billy had tried to draw a picture of Mr. Tooley with his walker, but he couldn't make it look right. So he took a new  piece of paper, folded it in half, and, on the front, drew the walker by itself on green, green grass to look like Mr. Tooley's lawn. Inside, he wrote the word *Sorry*, also in green.

Mama made brownies. When they had cooled, she cut them and wrapped them in foil. Then the three of them walked to Mr.

Tooley's house with the brownies and the sympathy cards. Sal had made six of them.

Because it was such a beautiful June day—the sky was as blue as Billy's new cerulean marker—they went the long way. They headed around the block in the opposite direction of Mr. Tooley's and wove through the neighborhood before heading back.

They passed Billy's best friend Ned's house.

"It looks sad," said Mama. It sounded like something Sal would say. But it was true.

The house was quiet. The windows were dark. The lawn was scruffy.

Ned was on a road trip with his family. They were driving throughout the Midwest. They'd left the day after the last day of school, and there was no firm plan as to when they'd return home to Wisconsin.

Ned was supposed to be sending postcards from interesting places. Ned's mother had said he needed to do this to practice his writing skills. But Billy hadn't received any yet.

Billy missed Ned. Ned hadn't been around for Billy's birthday. He hadn't seen the ambulance or the stretcher at Mr. Tooley's house. And now with Papa gone, too, Ned's absence was even more noticeable. Billy wondered if he'd be bored until one or the other of them came home.

Suddenly, Sal started waving excitedly at someone down the street.

It was Valerie Weaver, the neighborhood

letter carrier. She was striding toward them
with her big sack of mail. As she got closer,
her inky blue-black hair shone in the sun.

"Do you have something for me?" asked Sal.

"I don't think so," said Valerie.

"Is there something from Papa?" asked
Sal. "He went to art camp."

"Honey," said Mama. "Papa just left. He's
not even *at* art camp yet. He couldn't have
mailed anything so soon."

"Oh," murmured Sal.

"I like your headband," said Valerie.

Sal lovingly touched her headband and
adjusted it. "It's got ribbons and bows," she
said. "I'm like a flower!"

Something on Valerie's leg caught Sal's

attention. "Oh!" she said. "Look! Mama! A butterfly!" She reached out and touched the butterfly tattoo that was peeking out from beneath Valerie's sock.

Valerie bent over and pushed her sock down to reveal two more butterflies. "I just got them," said Valerie.

The butterflies were pink and blue. Two of them were about the size of a quarter. The other one was smaller—the size of a dime.

"A baby," said Sal, pointing at the littlest one. "Can I get a butterfly on my leg?"

"When you're eighteen," said Mama.

"I'm going to be four soon," Sal told Valerie.

Billy thought that if he'd ever get a tattoo, it would be a bat.

"Mr. Tooley died," said Sal.

"I heard that," said Valerie.

After a quiet moment, Valerie added, matter-of-factly, "People die every day and people are born every day. That's the way it is." She smiled and turned up the walkway to the nearest house with a handful of envelopes.

After Valerie had continued on her way, Billy could tell that Sal was trying to imitate Valerie's walk. Sal took long, stiff steps. One, two, three, four, five. Then she stopped, planting her feet.

"My feet are saying they're tired," said Sal. "Are we there yet?"

"Just about," said Mama. "Mr. Tooley's house is the yellow one. It's right there." She nodded to the little, low rectangular house with the green, green grass.

"Oh, the butter house," said Sal.

Mama laughed. "It does look like a stick of butter," she said. "Let's go."

As they approached the front door, a few thoughts occurred to Billy. Mama had told him that Mr. Tooley's grandson would be at the house. Billy wondered how old the grandson was and what grade he was in. Maybe he was going into third grade, too. Maybe he liked to play soccer.

It also occurred to Billy that he'd never been in the house of someone who'd just died. He wasn't sure how he felt about that.

# 6

Mr. Tooley's grandson was not going into third grade. Mr. Tooley's grandson was forty years old. He was older than Billy's parents. Billy was so surprised, it took a long moment for him to understand this, for it to sink in.

The grandson's name was Robert. Before Mama could ring the doorbell, Robert had come out onto the porch to greet them and introduce himself. He shook Billy's hand.

"Where's the grandson?" Billy whispered to Mama.

Robert heard Billy. "I'm the grandson," he said.

"But you're too old," said Billy softly.

"I can see why you'd think that," said Robert. "But my grandfather was very old. Ninety-two."

"How old are *you*?" Billy asked shyly.

"Forty," said Robert.

Billy didn't know grandchildren could be so old.

Mama gave Robert the brownies and the sympathy cards. Then Robert invited them into the house.

Billy worried that Mr. Tooley's house would

smell of a dead person, although he had no idea what that would actually smell like. Billy held his breath at first, and then he breathed through his mouth so that he wasn't able to smell anything. When he finally breathed normally, he realized that Mr. Tooley's house smelled like the old-fashioned hardware store with creaky floors that Papa liked to shop at. It was a good smell.

Robert and Mama were talking in calm voices about doctors and hospitals. Billy didn't listen. He gazed about the room. Mr. Tooley had more books than Billy had ever seen in someone's house. Billy felt as if he

were in a library. There were boxes—opened and closed—scattered around and stacked in the corner.

An older woman named Joan entered the room and joined them. She swayed a little when she walked—it was sort of like she was limping and sort of like she was dancing. Billy couldn't tell which it was. She was Mr. Tooley's daughter and Robert's mother. She said hello to everyone. She thanked Mama for the brownies. She admired Billy's card with Mr. Tooley's walker. Then she oohed and ahhed over Sal's sympathy cards.

"Your drawings are so pretty," Joan said. "They're the prettiest drawings I've ever seen."

Billy watched Sal watching Joan.

Joan clutched the drawings against her dress. "I love having these," she said.

Sal inched closer and closer to Joan.

Billy could tell that Sal had changed her mind. Now she did not want to part with her drawings. Billy could tell she wanted them back.

"Can I have my symphony cards back?" asked Sal.

Joan laughed. "Oh, sure. They're really pretty. I can see why you'd want to keep them."

"Sal—" Mama began.

Sal took the drawings from Joan and moved away. "I think they cheered you up

45

enough," said Sal. "I need them back because there are lots more dead people coming up. That's the way it is."

Joan laughed again. And so did Robert.

Mama didn't laugh. She smiled a tight-lipped smile. "Sal," she said, "when you give something to someone, it belongs to them."

"It's fine," said Joan. "It's fine." She motioned to Sal to keep the drawings.

Robert laughed again. "That's the way it is."

It struck Billy that Joan should have been happy to have *his* drawing. She hadn't made such a fuss over his sympathy card even though he was a much better artist than Sal. Maybe, thought Billy, Joan was just trying to be nice to a little kid.

"Maybe Sal could keep *one*," suggested Billy. He was trying to be helpful with Sal as Papa had told him to be. "Or the lady could keep one."

Sal and Joan said *no* at the exact same time. Sal's *no* was mournful; Joan's was almost jolly.

"No, no," Joan added. She smiled, and because her mouth was big, her smile was enormous.

Mama sighed. "We need to go," she said. "We have things to do." She scooped up Sal and crossed the room to the door.

Billy followed.

Outside, Mama set Sal down. Neither Mama, Sal, nor Billy spoke. They walked wordlessly down the sidewalk. It felt like the hallway at school when no one is supposed to talk.

Sal broke the silence. "What are the things to do?" she asked.

Mama kept up her pace, which was brisk. "Seeing all those boxes gave me an idea," she said. "We're going to clean the basement. It will be a nice surprise for Papa."

The basement was the coolest place in the house. Billy could feel the temperature change as he walked down the stairs. He went up and down a few times just to feel the sensation. It was like magic.

He tried to find the exact spot where half his body was cold and half was hot. He was standing on the steps, arms outstretched, moving a bit this way, moving a bit that way.

"What are you doing?" asked Sal.

"Nothing," said Billy, dropping his arms.

"Were you a bird?" she asked.

"No."

"An airplane?"

"No."

It wasn't unusual for Sal to interrupt Billy when he was having a perfectly satisfactory private moment. If he remembered, he'd try this again later when he was alone.

"What are you *doing*?" Sal asked again.

Billy jumped from where he was on the stairs to the cement basement floor. "What I'm doing is helping Mama clean the basement," he said.

Mama looked like she meant business. She'd stuffed her thick hair into one of Papa's baseball caps and pulled the cap low over her eyes. And she was wearing one of Papa's old plaid work shirts. The fabric was as thin as tissue paper. The cuffs were frayed, and there were little holes running along many of the seams. Sal made a game of rushing up to Mama, poking her finger through one of the holes, and saying, "Peek-a-boo!"

The air in the basement was heavy and damp. In the corners, cobwebs hung from the ceiling in clotted strands. This, thought Billy, is like the human version of a bat cave. Bats were on his mind because he was wearing his new bat T-shirt. He usually didn't pay much attention to clothes, but this was definitely his favorite shirt. He wondered how many days he could wear it before Mama made him throw it down the laundry chute. He'd try to keep it clean.

"What a mess," Mama said. She looked around and said it again, "What a mess."

Billy didn't think the basement was messy. In fact, he thought it was fairly tidy. It's not that there wasn't a lot of stuff—there was. But that didn't seem like a problem to Billy.

The big main room they were in had unpainted cinder-block walls and roughly made wooden shelves. The shelves were crammed and overflowing with all kinds of things.

There were flowerpots, dishes, magazines, and

record albums. There were buckets of paint-brushes, rusty paint cans, extension cords, and coils of rope. There were many boxes that Mama said were filled with letters, clothes, books, and old photographs. There were other things on the floor: hockey sticks,  baseball bats, a warped tennis racket, a rake, a shovel, a shabby suitcase, a sew-ing machine, and an old-fashioned baby buggy.

"It looks good to me," said Billy.

Mama laughed. "Sometimes I wish I could see the world through your eyes, Billy Miller," she said.

"What about *my* eyes?" asked Sal.

"Your eyes are beautiful," said Mama.

"My eyes are beautiful," said Sal.

Mama got right to work. She started pulling things off the shelves. She opened a few boxes and looked inside. She'd sniff or make a funny face or smile and then move on to the next one.

"We'll make three piles," said Mama. "Things to keep, things to donate, and things to throw away."

Billy's job was to help move the boxes and other items Mama had placed on the floor out to the middle of the room. Then they would sort everything. Some boxes were light and easy to carry. Some were heavy, and Billy had to push them.

After a few minutes, Billy took notice.

The shelves were half-empty. Boxes, some opened, some not, and a random assortment of household goods were scattered across the floor, roughly concentrated in the center of the room. *Now* it's messy, thought Billy.

"Special delivery!" yelled Sal. "I'm Valerie, the mail person." Sal was pushing the baby buggy. She'd move it forward a few feet, stop, pretend to take something out, and toss it into the air.

Each time she stopped, she named a different recipient. "Special delivery for the Drip Sisters! Special delivery for Papa! Special delivery for Mr. Tooley!" she said. "Oops, I forgot he's dead."

"She's not helping," Billy said to Mama.

"That's okay," said Mama. "Sometimes, it's easier if she's not." Mama smiled in that knowing way that made Billy feel grown up, as if he were included in an adult secret.

Mama got very interested in one of the boxes. She pulled folded pieces of paper from envelopes in the box, read some, and replaced them. She laughed at what she read; she sighed. At one point, she stared off into space, pressing one of the envelopes to her shirt.

Billy had gotten interested in some board games he had never seen before. They looked ancient. They were probably from when Mama and Papa were little.

Sal had picked up speed. She tripped over one of the coils of rope and lurched forward.

The baby buggy rammed into the shelving. A clay pot fell to the floor, breaking into several pieces. And then Sal screamed, and covered her head, not because of the broken pot, but because a bat shot out from the darkness behind the shelves and flew into the room, swooping around and around, close to the walls.

"Wow," said Billy, completely mesmerized. He wanted to get a better, closer look at the bat, but he couldn't move. He was as still as a statue.

"Oh boy," said Mama. "I don't like this. Billy, take Sal and go upstairs. Close the door to the basement behind you."

"What are you—" Billy began.

"Go, go," said Mama. "I'm going to open

the window and hopefully it will fly out."

The bat was circling like a small dusky machine that wouldn't stop.

Billy led Sal out of the basement and up the stairs to the back hall. Before he closed the door, he turned around and listened. He couldn't tell what was happening. Part of him wanted to sneak back downstairs. But he didn't.

"Are bats good or bad?" asked Sal.

"Good," said Billy. "I think. They eat mosquitoes."

"I don't like mosquitoes," said Sal. "I don't think I like bats, either."

"I do," said Billy.

"Maybe the bat came because of your shirt," said Sal.

Billy glanced down at the bat on his T-shirt.

"Maybe it's your fault," said Sal.

Billy was overcome by an odd feeling. He *had* been thinking about bats because of his shirt. Had his birthday wish for something exciting to happen caused *this*? *Was* it his fault? Did he have some strange new power? He thought he'd gotten over his feelings about Mr. Tooley's death, but now he wasn't so sure.

While they waited for Mama to return from the basement, Billy ran up to his room. He changed his shirt. He put on a plain gray T-shirt. He rolled the bat T-shirt into a ball and shoved it under his bed, as far into the dusty darkness as possible.

# 8

"Well, I'm glad that's over," said Mama. "I hope nothing else exciting happens."

"Me, too," said Billy. *Exciting.* There was that word from his birthday wish again. No more excitement, thought Billy. Please.

Mama, Billy, and Sal were driving to the grocery store.

"Will the bat man come back?" asked Sal.

"I hope not," said Mama. "I hope he won't have to."

Mama had called a man named Nate to come and check the house for bats. He'd arrived in a silver truck that said "Bat Man" in big letters on the door. Under that it said "Bat Control & Removal."

Billy liked Nate because Nate liked bats. "Bats are awesome," said Nate.

Nate walked through the basement and all around the outside of the house. Then he got a ladder from his truck and went up on the roof to inspect it and the chimney to see if there were any places where a bat could have entered the house.

"Everything seems good and tight," yelled Nate. "So far."

While Nate was on the roof, Mama called

Papa. She told him about the bat. Billy could hear Mama's voice change. It got lighter and happier as the conversation went on. "Really?" she said. "That's good. Oh, good. I'll tell the bat man."

Both Billy and Sal wanted to talk to Papa. But Mama leaned away from them and shook her head. "You can talk to him tonight," she whispered.

"What did Papa say?" asked Billy when Mama hung up. "What's good?"

"Well," said Mama. "Papa told me that last night he propped the back door open while he was getting some things out of the basement for his trip. He said the door was open for about fifteen minutes. He thinks the bat must have flown in then and couldn't get out after Papa closed the door when he was done." Mama smiled. "It makes sense to me," she said. "I'll tell Nate."

It made sense to Nate, too. "Everything seems fine on the roof," said Nate. "No gaps, no irregularities, no problems. I have a feeling you had one lost, lonely little bat. End of story."

I hope it is the end of the story, thought Billy as they pulled into the grocery store parking lot. He decided that as much as he liked bats, he now preferred them outside.

Sal loved going to the grocery store because she liked to bring the Drip Sisters to the produce section and play with them under the misters that kept the lettuce and other vegetables fresh.

"It's raining on the Drip Sisters," she'd say, delighted. "The girls love rain. Because they're drips."

As they walked across the parking lot to the store entrance, Mama asked a favor of Billy. "Honey, would you mind taking Sal to the rain? I'll hurry through and get what we need. I'm a little tired. If you help me by doing this, we can get home faster."

"Sure," said Billy. He rarely thought of Mama as being tired during the day. The thought circled like a bat, but he didn't dwell on it.

The air was humid and thick with the scent of oranges and what Billy called the grocery store smell.

"I hope it's raining a lot," Sal said eagerly.

"Be patient," Mama said to Sal. "And be good for Billy." Mama raised her eyebrows and smiled at Billy. "And you be patient, too," she said in a quiet voice.

Inside, Mama grabbed a cart and rushed off. Billy grabbed Sal's hand and headed for the produce section.

The misters turned off just as Billy and Sal approached the long wall lined with lettuce, cabbage, celery, parsley, broccoli, and several things Billy wasn't very familiar with: chard, fennel, kale, kohlrabi.

"The rain turned off," Sal said, obviously disappointed.

"It'll come back on," said Billy. "Remember, be patient."

While she was waiting, Sal lined up the five Drip Sisters on the flat metal edging that bordered the vegetable bins. "We're ready," said Sal. "Hurry up, rain."

"Need help?" asked a man who worked at the store. He seemed old to Billy, at least thirty. He was wearing a long green apron and a green baseball cap tipped sideways.

"We're waiting for the rain," said Sal.

Billy could feel his cheeks redden. "My sister likes to watch when the water sprays down on the vegetables," Billy explained. "She calls it rain."

"Oh," said the man. "Cute." He shrugged. "Well, those things go on and off all day.

You wait long enough, they'll start up." He shrugged again and walked away.

"Sometimes you have to wait for the rain," Sal told the Drip Sisters in a breezy fashion. "Be patient."

Nothing happened.

The seconds seemed like hours to Billy. He could tell that Sal was quickly growing impatient. She was shifting from one foot to the other. She sighed dramatically.

"Be patient," Billy reminded her.

"If it doesn't rain soon," said Sal, "we'll have to start singing."

"I'm not singing," said Billy.

"Papa does," said Sal. "He sings 'Raindrops Keep Fallin' on My Head.' He says it makes the rain come faster. The song goes like this—"

Oh no, thought Billy.

Sal began singing, "Raindrops keep falling on my head. . . ."

As if by magic, the misters turned on. First there was a clicking sound, then a wheezing noise, and then the soft, whispery *shush-shushing* of the misters going full force.

"Rain!" said Sal. "Now you make them dance." She picked up two of the Drip Sisters and moved them through the mist. "Help me, Billy," she said. "You have to give each one a turn before the rain shuts off."

Billy did not want to do this, but he also did not want the misters to turn off before each Drip Sister had had a turn. He grabbed one and jerkily raised and lowered it.

"More gentle," said Sal. "They're *dancing*. Not jumping."

Billy conceded. Grudgingly, he made smooth, graceful loops with one of the Drip Sisters. He closed his eyes in an attempt to make himself disappear, to make everything disappear.

"Hello, Billy," said an oddly familiar voice. "How nice to see you."

Billy turned around. Oh no, he thought.

It was Ms. Silver, Billy's second grade teacher. She was pushing a stroller with one

69

hand and holding a basket for groceries with the other. Oranges and bananas were in the basket. A sleeping baby was in the stroller.

Billy froze. He let out a nearly silent strangled groan. He was standing in front of his former teacher holding a cute little whale eraser in midair. Ms. Silver must have seen him "dancing" it around. He lowered his arm and tried to hide the Drip Sister.

He looked at her helplessly, then looked away. His mind was swirling with horrible thoughts: *I am such a baby. I am a complete and total idiot.*

Billy tried to explain. "I'm watching my sister while my mom shops. She has these little erasers and she likes to play with them in the—" He didn't know how to make this understandable, to make it clear.

He didn't have to. Ms. Silver smiled broadly. "You're such a good big brother," she told him. "That doesn't surprise me. It doesn't surprise me at all."

Just like that, Billy swelled with a pleasant feeling. His eyes connected with Ms. Silver's, then darted off.

"Oh, by the way," said Ms. Silver, "this is Carson." She'd been moving the stroller back and forth while they'd been talking. "If I stop, he'll wake up."

"Nice," said Billy. Carson looked like an ordinary baby. Kind of big. Nothing special.

"Well," said Ms. Silver, "I should do my

shopping. Have a great summer, Billy."

"Bye," said Billy. It was strange to see Ms. Silver somewhere other than school. He thought that teachers weren't regular people. They were in a different category—like doctors or presidents. They existed in a world separate from the world in which he lived. He knew this wasn't true, but it felt true. Billy watched Ms. Silver as she merged into a ribbon of other shoppers leaving the produce section.

Sal was still making the Drip Sisters dance in the rain. She probably hadn't even noticed Ms. Silver.

All of a sudden, the misters turned off.

"Oh no," said Sal.

"Remember, be patient," said Billy. "The rain will start again, you'll see."

He started humming "Raindrops Keep Fallin' on My Head" very, very softly. That much he could do.

He stared at the lettuce while he waited. Droplets of water covered the leaves like diamonds or beads of mercury. He let his vision blur. The droplets glistened and shimmered. They turned into a silvery-white smear. And,  then, suddenly, everything became sharp again as the misters came on once more, and Mama returned with two frosted doughnuts with sprinkles. One for Sal and one for Billy.

# 9

That night Billy talked to Papa on the telephone. Billy told Papa about the bat. He tried to explain how amazing it had been to see a bat close up. He also explained that it had been a little scary, too.

Before Billy could ask Papa about art camp, he found himself getting sad. Hearing Papa's voice made Billy miss him, so he said goodbye quickly and passed the phone back to Mama.

In bed, he couldn't stop thinking about Papa, which kept him from sleeping. Then he started thinking about Mr. Tooley to keep his mind off Papa. That wasn't helpful. Now he couldn't get an image of Mr. Tooley with milky eyes, bushy white eyebrows, sunken cheeks, and wrinkled papery skin out of his head.

Finally he fell asleep. In the morning, he had no memory of his restless night, it was one day closer to Papa coming home, and—he could smell pancakes in the kitchen.

"Your pancakes are almost as good as Papa's," said Sal cheerfully.

Mama laughed. "Thank you."

"I think they are *exactly* as good," said Billy.

Mama smiled at him.

"Papa makes shapes," said Sal.

"Well, that makes sense," said Mama. "He's an artist."

"You're a *teacher*," said Sal.

Hearing the word *teacher* made Billy think of Ms. Silver, which made him think of school, which made him think of third grade. Thankfully, it was the start of summer vacation, so third grade was a long, long, long time away.

Billy ate slowly. At this very moment, he was happy. He was thinking that summer lay before him like an endless highway. Once his friend Ned came home from his trip and Papa returned, he could settle into a comfortable summer. He could really start to have fun.

Billy could feel the sun shining through  the window and spilling across the table. Out the window the sky was bright blue. There wasn't a cloud in sight. He was quietly taking it all in when he felt something else, something like the sun, but different.

He looked up. It was Mama. She was watching him. "What?" he asked.

"Nothing," she said. She made a funny gesture with her hand, as if holding back the air, then she kissed Billy's head. Sal's, too. "You're both growing up so fast. Sometimes it seems like you're changing right in front of me." She rumpled Billy's unruly hair.

Billy squirmed, his lips tightening. He didn't like it when adults got thoughtful and mushy about growing up the way they often did. He didn't think *he* would ever do that. He *wanted* to be grown up. To be as tall as Papa. To be able to drive. To be able to do whatever he wanted to do all day long.

While he finished his pancakes, Mama told Billy and Sal that she'd changed her mind about the basement. She'd decided that they'd just put everything back on the shelves, tidy up, sweep the floor, and deal with sorting through everything when Papa was home. "I don't think I have the energy to tackle this project right now," she said. "Maybe the bat did me in."

Minutes later her plan changed again. "I have a new idea," she said. Would Billy take Sal down to the basement, start working on putting things away, and watch Sal while she lay down for a few minutes?

"I hate naps," said Sal.

"Are you okay?" asked Billy.

"Yes," said Mama. "Just tired. I got up really early. And I think a whole year of teaching is catching up with me. I'm glad it's vacation," she added. She shrugged and smiled in a relaxed and easygoing manner as if to say *no big deal.*

"Maybe I can use Billy's markers," said Sal.

"Maybe," said Mama. She shared a secret glance with Billy. *That might not be a bad idea*, she mouthed. She wiped the counter with a dishcloth, then draped the cloth over the edge of the sink. She turned back toward Billy and Sal, her face breaking into a coaxing, slanted grin that dented one of her cheeks. "Maybe we can go out for dinner tonight for a treat," she said. As she left the kitchen, she added, "I'll come and check in with you in no time. No time at all."

Billy looked at Sal. She was pretending to have the Drip Sisters drink, one by one, from the puddle of syrup on her plate. When it comes to watching Sal, no time at all can feel like a very long time, thought Billy.

# 10

In the basement, the mess from yesterday was laid out before them like the aftermath of a tornado. The thought of putting everything back where it belonged was overwhelming to Billy. But he wanted to help Mama. He turned his head from side to side, looking at the clutter with glazed eyes and a questioning frown.

"What are we going to play?" asked Sal.

"We're not supposed to play," said Billy. "We're supposed to work."

"I'm going to be Valerie," said Sal. "I'm a mail person." She hurried over to the baby buggy with outstretched arms and a gleeful expression.

"No," said Billy, blocking her path. "No yelling 'special delivery.' And no pushing the buggy into things like you did before." He was fairly confident that there were no more bats, but still, he didn't want her carelessly plowing into the shelves again, making noise, stirring things up.

Sal wrinkled her nose at Billy. "I could use your markers."

He didn't want to let her use his markers yet. He wanted to keep them as a last resort. "I think there's a box of letters here somewhere. You could organize them and put them in the buggy."

"That doesn't sound like fun," said Sal.

"You could deliver them later. I think mail people do that—organize letters."

Sal blinked her eyes as if each blink were helping her process his suggestions.

"We have to be quiet for Mama," said Billy. "And organizing mail would make you an official mail person," he added. "Official is good."

Blink.

"Official means you are the real thing."

Blink. Blink.

"They're *real* letters with *real* stamps."

Blink. Blink. Blink.

"Okay," she said. "But I get to deliver them soon."

"Yes," said Billy, nodding.

Billy found the box of letters and dragged it over to Sal. Quickly, she got to work. She sank to her knees and began making piles.

First she separated the letters by size. Then she placed all the colored envelopes together. She picked out the envelopes with postage stamps she particularly liked and put them in the buggy first.

She talked as she sorted, her soft, clear voice rising and falling as if she were chirping a song. Billy couldn't make out what she was saying, but she was busy—that was what mattered.

He tried to work quickly, too. He put the least heavy boxes and objects on the shelves first. He soon realized that the space on the shelves was disappearing fast, but the floor was still filled with clutter. He also realized that the shelves had been tightly packed; everything had fit together like pieces of a puzzle. Another realization: it had been much easier to pull things off the shelves than it was to replace them.

Billy was growing frustrated. With a knuckle in his mouth he circled the room. He wasn't doing a very good job and he knew it.

"Okay," said Sal suddenly. "I'm ready for markers. If you don't let me, I'll go ask Mama."

"No," said Billy firmly. "No."

"I'll draw quietly," she said. "I have a really good idea. It will be the real thing. And I won't bother you at all."

Silence.

"I won't yell 'special delivery.'"

Silence.

"I won't look for Mama."

"Okay," said Billy. "You win."

"What did I win?" asked Sal, beaming.

Billy rolled his eyes. "It means you get to use my markers."

# 11

Making as little noise as possible, Billy went up to his bedroom to get his markers and some paper. He set them out for Sal on the floor in the corner of the big main room of the basement. She settled in right away. She sat with her back to him and said over her shoulder, "You can't watch me. It's a surprise."

"Fine," he said, feeling annoyed. Although he thought it was probably better *not* to watch anyway. He didn't want to torture himself by witnessing his markers possibly being ruined.

But the good thing was that Sal was quiet. Very quiet. So Billy returned to the task at hand.

It didn't take Billy long to lose steam. Halfheartedly he pushed some boxes around and shoved others with his feet, but he wasn't making real progress. He got sidetracked by looking inside some of the boxes. Then he wandered into the dark, shadowy room taken up  by the furnace, the water heater, and a network of pipes that ran along the ceiling and up and down the walls.

When Billy was little, he was certain that something evil lived in the furnace room. Or, worse, that the room itself was alive, exposing its creaky, creepy, private insides. The smell of it, the sound of it, the feel of it—all of it—had convinced him of this.

It was Papa who had helped Billy get over his fear of the furnace room. With the dim single lightbulb turned on overhead and two flashlights (one for each of them) shining, Papa had led Billy through the room explaining how and why things worked and what the noises actually were.

"When we turn on the heat upstairs," Papa had said, "the igniter on the furnace makes that clicking sound you were talking about.

And the toilet flushing makes a whooshing sound."

Papa had yelled upstairs, asking Mama to flush the toilet. "Now listen," Papa had said. "You'll hear it."

The water rushed through the pipes like a terrifying, raging river. Using his flashlight, Papa indicated the path of the water. Billy followed the bouncing shaft of light as it traveled around the room, tracing the pipes. He felt surrounded by the noise. It was everywhere, but it wasn't scary any longer because he understood it.

"I still don't like the smell," Billy had said.

"I think it smells like rain in here," Papa had said. "Try to think of it that way. Rain is nice."

One by one, Papa had addressed Billy's worries until they'd fizzled. Until they were gone.

Now, it still was not Billy's favorite room in the house, but it didn't scare him. It was just a room. He smiled to himself as he stood on the threshold thinking of Papa. He wondered how art camp was going.

It suddenly occurred to Billy that he hadn't heard a peep from Sal. Which was highly unusual.

He left the furnace room and crept toward her, keeping a safe distance. She appeared busy, engrossed, hunched over whatever she was working on. But, curiously, the stack of paper beside her seemed neat and untouched. He thought by now she'd have run out of paper and that her drawings would be scattered across the floor.

Billy was suspicious. He inched closer. Closer.

He stopped. She still hadn't noticed him. He was directly behind her now. He leaned to one side and craned his neck. "Sal!" he said, his eyes widening.

Sal jerked around. "What?"

"What are you *doing*?"

"I'm making tattoos. Just like Valerie. Now I can be the real thing. I can deliver the mail when I'm done."

"Sal!" he said again, bewildered, because he didn't know what else to say.

"Valerie only has three butterflies. I have *millions*!"

Sal didn't have millions, but she had a lot. Sal's legs were covered, from her ankles to her knees, with what looked to Billy like colorful blobs and squiggles, but to Sal were butterflies.

"Mama said I had to wait till I was eighteen," said Sal. "But I did it myself."

Yeah, you did it, thought Billy. You really did it. He picked up a marker, turning it in his hand to read the label. He put it down and picked up another. And another. He picked up the black marker Sal had been using. Reading the label caused his breath to catch. "Oh no," he said.

"What?" said Sal. She was tilting her head

and turning her outstretched legs, admiring them. Her smile was toothy.

"The black one's permanent," said Billy.

"What's that mean?"

"It means it won't wash off."

"Good," said Sal. "I like my butterfly tattoos."

"But they're *not* good. They don't even look professional. They look like a baby scribbled all over your legs."

Sal took a deep breath. She traced over one of her butterflies with her finger. "You don't like them?" she asked.

"Who cares if I like them," said Billy. "They're *permanent*."

"Permanent?" she whispered.

"Don't you understand?" said Billy. "Don't you get it? Permanent means you're going to have ugly black marks on your legs forever. Even if you live to be one hundred."

Judging by Sal's sunken face, she understood.

It was so quiet even the furnace room was silent.

Sal licked her finger and rubbed one of the butterflies. The blue and green wings smeared, but the black outline did not. She licked her finger again and rubbed harder. The color was nearly gone. The black was unchanged.

Then Sal pulled her legs up and tried to cover them by wrapping her arms around them. Her knees were under her chin. She seemed to be trying to make herself smaller, drawing inward. She looked at Billy. Her eyes were shining with welled-up tears and probed his as if to say *How, oh how, will you fix this?*

"I don't like this," Sal said in a thin, squeaky voice. She started rocking, back and forth, back and forth.

Billy knew this was not good. Sal's rocking was often accompanied, first, by whimpering, then by full-fledged, very loud crying. He chewed on his lower lip until he tasted blood.

He tried to think of something to do. Something that would keep Sal from throwing a fit. Something that would keep Mama from being disturbed.

He knew that on the high shelf by the basement sink Mama and Papa kept a bottle of bleach and a canister of powdered cleanser along with other things that were dangerous, even poisonous. Maybe they would remove the black marker. But he wasn't allowed to touch them, and he didn't think Mama would want him to do that even in an emergency. Too risky.

He thought of taking one of the Drip Sisters and hiding it. He could pretend it was missing to create a distraction for Sal. After a while, he could "find it." Then maybe she'd be so happy that she'd forget about her tattoos. Unlikely.

Sal was rocking ferociously now, as if she were riding a sea of despair, facing wave upon wave of dread.

Billy could think of nothing to do but make sure the door to upstairs was closed. He did that, then he prepared himself for the inevitable crying by balling his hand into fists, squeezing his eyes shut, and standing as still as stone.

The tears came. They came and came. Sal swiped at them and licked them from her splotchy pink cheeks. At first her crying was quiet, but gradually it escalated until it was very loud, and then so loud that Billy knew that Mama would have to be wearing extra-powerful earplugs not to hear it.

"Shh," Billy murmured. It did no good, but he continued. "Shh. Shh. You'll wake Mama."

And then like a shaft of light, Mama's voice broke into the room. "I'm awake."

# 12

Mama came to them with a lot of questions, but they were asked with such calmness, the room seemed to settle and shrink.

Mama asked: "What's wrong?" and "Is everyone okay?" and "What happened?"

While Billy explained everything, Sal collapsed into Mama with complete abandon. They huddled together on the floor. Billy watched Mama run her hands over Sal's legs. When Sal had stopped shaking, she pulled away from Mama a bit and looked at her with sad, red-rimmed, rabbity eyes. "Will you fix it?" she asked. Her voice was tight, caught in her throat. "Will I be permanent forever?"

Mama laughed gently. "No, sweetie," she said. "It's okay. Everything is okay. Remember, things usually aren't as bad as you think they are."

"Are you mad?" asked Sal, trembling again.

Billy waited for Mama's response without breathing. Because this had happened on his watch, he felt partially responsible.

"Of course not," said Mama.

That's good, thought Billy.

"What's going to happen?" asked Sal.

"The label says permanent," Billy offered, trying to be helpful. "Look," he said, holding up the marker for Mama to see. He thought it was important information. Proof.

Mama nodded to Billy, then turned back to Sal. "Your legs are very colorful," she said. "Are you sure you don't want to keep them the way they are for a while? You could show Papa when he comes home."

"No!" said Sal. "They're ugly."

"Well," said Mama, "then we'll do a little scrubbing. Maybe a lot. Don't worry."

"Will it hurt?" asked Sal.

"No," said Mama.

"Will there be a happy ending?" asked Sal.

Mama smiled. "Yes."

For a while, though, it seemed there would be no happy ending.

First Mama tried to clean up Sal's legs with regular soap and water in the bathtub. That worked a little.

Next Mama tried scrubbing a mixture of salt and water on Sal's legs with a washcloth. That worked a bit better.

Then Mama tried rubbing alcohol. That worked best. The rubbing alco-hol didn't return Sal's legs to their natural condition, but Billy thought they looked pretty good. Now there were spidery, purplish marks covering them, but the marks were faint.

Billy wouldn't say it out loud, but part of him was a little disappointed that the marker wasn't really permanent. He thought it was false advertising. What he *did* say was that Sal's legs looked like they had crooked crossword puzzles printed all over them. This was not a good thing to say. Sal started crying again.

Billy tried once more. "Well, Sal you look kind of tough. Like you were in a fight and got all bruised up."

That wasn't helpful, either. Billy decided that he would never be a parent. It was too hard, and it would take too much time away from doing fun things for yourself.

Mama was helpful. She reminded Sal about the lump Billy had gotten last year when he fell while they were on vacation. "Remember," said Mama, "how Billy thought his lump would never go away. And, then, one day, he realized it was gone. I think it'll be like that. Your beautiful purple tattoos will wear off. Maybe you'll even miss them," Mama added, smiling.

Sal squinted, considering this. The circles under her eyes matched the marks on her legs in color. She filled her cheeks with air like a puffer fish. She let her breath out slowly.

Billy touched his head. He hadn't thought about his lump in a while. "Mama's right," he said. "You'd never even know I had a lump."

Sal buried her face in Mama's lap. "I'm *still* not happy," she squeaked.

"I have an idea," said Mama.

Mama left the basement and returned a few minutes later carrying a bag. She gave the bag to Sal. "I was saving this for your birthday," said Mama. "But I think you should have it now."

"What is it?" asked Sal.

"You'll see," said Mama. "Look."

Sal opened the bag and pulled out a pair of brightly colored tights. "Oh!" said Sal.

"Do you like them?" asked Mama.

"Yes!" was Sal's answer. "There's even butterflies!"

The tights were patterned with butterflies and flowers and bees and birds. The tights were blue and pink and green and yellow and orange and purple.

Sal was in such a hurry to pull on her new tights, they bunched up and she nearly fell over.

"Hold on," said Mama. "I'll help you."

When they had successfully gotten the tights in place, Sal said, "Now I'm not crying."

"Happy ending?" said Mama, brushing Sal's hair off her forehead.

Sal nodded. She kept looking down at her tights. One long, last shudder rippled through her as if her body were ridding itself of the bad experience for good.

"Your legs kind of look like they have tattoos on them," Billy said to Sal. "Only now they look professional."

"And I can take them off when I want to," said Sal. "Or I can keep them on forever."

Sal's energy had drained away, but now it was restored. She marched around the room proudly and joyfully.

That night when they called Papa, enough time had passed that everyone seemed to find the tattoo incident funny and interesting.

"It sounds like you're having an exciting time without me," Papa said to Billy. There was that word again: *exciting*. He was starting to hate it. Was it possible to hate a word?

"Are you having fun, Papa?" asked Billy.

"Yes. I'm learning glassblowing and welding. You'd like it."

Neither spoke for a moment, then Papa said, "Hey, did you forget?"

"Forget what?"

"I thought you were calling me Dad."

"Oh yeah," said Billy. "Well, it's hard for me to remember."

"Not a problem. I like Papa. I'm used to it."

"Maybe I could have until the end of the summer," said Billy. "After that I'll call you Dad."

"Sounds like a plan," said Papa.

Before Billy could say goodbye, Sal grabbed the phone, and so Billy drifted away and drifted around the yard.

The warm night air felt like a blanket of softness. All around the trees were dark, like a border hemming the sky. It seemed to Billy that the day had been a long one—it felt like a year. And it seemed as if Papa had been gone forever.

# 13

The next day was uneventful, which suited Billy just fine. No sirens, no dead people, no bats, no tattoos.

Billy and Mama finished putting the basement back in order. When they were done, Mama took Billy and Sal to the public pool for the first time this summer.

If Billy were trying to imagine a perfect summer day, this was it. The day was sunny and bright, the air was hot and clear, the sky was blue and cloudless.

Right away, at the pool, Billy noticed that the twisty slide had been replaced. The new one was taller, had more twists, and—as Billy discovered when he tried it out—was smoother and therefore faster.

The wait to go down the slide was long, but it was worth it. There was a moment when Billy left the slide but hadn't hit the water yet—he was airborne. That moment was the best. But the sensation of plunging into the cool water was almost as thrilling.

Sal didn't want to go on the slide; she wanted to play in the little kids' pool. Mama sat at the side of the pool in a recliner and kept an eye on her. Billy was grateful he didn't have to watch her.

Sal was wearing her new tights with her bathing suit. She'd worn the tights to bed the night before, too. Billy thought she looked goofy. He pretended she wasn't his sister.

Billy ran into some friends from school— Jordan Johnson and Calvin Maloney. They made waiting in line more fun. Billy told them about the bat and that he had been in the house of a newly dead person. Jordan and Calvin were sufficiently impressed.

Standing beneath the slide, inching along, looking up at it, gave Billy a feeling of quiet astonishment. The slide was truly majestic; it kind of took his breath away. He wondered if anyone else ever felt this way about a waterslide.

For Mama, it was books and nature that made her especially happy in this way. For Papa, it was tools and gadgets and big metal sculptures in public parks that looked to Billy like a giant had taken rusty beams and tossed them carelessly to the ground.

After going down the slide so many times he lost track, Billy was so hungry he could barely stand it. Surprisingly, Mama let Billy and Sal eat lunch at the pool snack bar, which she usually didn't do because she didn't think they served healthy food. Happily, Billy ordered a macaroni and cheese bowl (to which he added ten squirts of ketchup and two squirts of mustard from the big jugs on the counter), a bag of potato chips, apple juice, and a root beer Popsicle for dessert.

Afterward everyone was a little sleepy, and so they went home. Driving through the neighborhood, they saw Valerie, the mail carrier.

Sal lowered her window. "I've got tattoos!" she yelled. "But they're really tights!"

Valerie smiled and waved.

Billy ducked beneath the window until they had passed by Valerie. Sal was so embarrassing.

Seeing Valerie must have reminded Sal about the buggy in the basement. "Can I deliver mail when we get home?" asked Sal. "Can I use the buggy? Can I go around the block?"

"Yes, yes, yes," Mama answered. "As long as Billy goes with you."

"Goody!" said Sal.

Goody, thought Billy, making a horrid face.

Luckily Mama didn't see it. She was keeping her eyes on the road.

The buggy was surprisingly light, but it was still awkward dragging it up the basement stairs. Somehow Billy managed to get it up the stairs and out the back door by himself. He noticed that the buggy was still stuffed with letters from one of the boxes from the basement. Billy shook his head.

He did not want to pretend to deliver mail with his weird little sister who was wearing tights in blazing hot weather. He wondered how long he had to do things like this. How long big brothers had to suffer because of their little sisters.

Billy waited for Sal by the back door. He waited and waited and waited. He doubted that she'd forgotten about delivering the mail, seeing how excited she'd been about doing it.

He went inside and found her in the living room curled up like a little cat beside Mama on the couch. Both were sleeping.

Billy sighed—a big, long sigh of relief. For now, at least, he was spared of his brotherly responsibilities. Quietly he left them alone and went up to his room.

As soon as he crossed the threshold, Billy sensed his room darken as if an invisible hand had pulled down the window shade. Then he heard the soft beginning of rainfall on the roof.

He went to the window and looked out over the yard. The rain was gentle, but steady. In intervals, the rain increased, shifting through the yard in sheets. Billy saw the buggy. He ran downstairs and out into the rain. He put the buggy in the garage.

After toweling off, Billy went back to his room. He finally had time alone with his markers. Billy lay on the floor beside a pile of paper and his markers arranged in a fan. He barely had to think what to draw. While the rain drummed down, Billy drew the world's tallest waterslide, complete with complicated turns, tunnels, and a jump so wide you were airborne for ten whole seconds—which is a very long time if you actually timed it.

The rain continued. It rained all afternoon, through the night, and for most of the next morning. When it finally stopped, the sky was milky, and then the sun broke through the haziness and the day turned hot and sticky.

After lunch Sal wanted to get the buggy from the garage and pretend to be Valerie and deliver mail. She had her tights on, of course, and she was ready to go.

"Are you ever going to take those off?" asked Billy.

"When the permanent marker goes away," said Sal. She tugged down her shorts and then her tights to check her legs. "Still there," she said.

Billy looked at Mama with an expression that said: *Do I really have to do this? Please, please, please don't make me do this.*

Mama smiled sympathetically at Billy and gave him a hug with an extra squeeze. "Just go once around the block. It'll be over in no time," she said softly.

"Can you tell her no shouting 'special delivery'?" asked Billy.

Mama nodded.

"Can you tell her to go really fast?"

Mama nodded again. She had a little talk with Sal, and then Sal and Billy were on their way.

As they started off, the wind picked up and droplets of rain that had collected in the leaves of the trees overhead showered down on them.

Billy looked up hopefully to see if it was starting to rain again. If it was, they could turn back. But it wasn't. And it seemed improbable that Sal would have turned back now even if it were pouring.

With a bit of a swagger Sal marched down the sidewalk pushing the buggy. Billy kept a safe distance. "Remember, no yelling," he told her. "We're going once around the block. And we're going fast."

"Mail!" said Sal.

"Quieter," said Billy.

They went down the street, stopping at

each house. Billy stayed on the main sidewalk and Sal pushed the buggy up each smaller walkway to the front door where the mailbox was. Billy waited, turned away, pretending to do other things—checking for traffic, coughing, examining his fingernails, patting his pockets as if he'd lost something.

Because he wasn't really paying attention, he couldn't say for certain what Sal was actually doing or what she was saying. Out of the corner of his eye, he caught glimpses of her gesturing, waving envelopes around. And he heard snatches of her talking to imaginary people—nothing he could understand—and then the *thunk* of mailboxes shutting.

"We're delivering mail," Sal said with glee.

"*I'm* not," muttered Billy.

Luckily they only saw a few people. Mrs. Metcalf was walking her little fluffy dog, Winker. Mrs. Metcalf smiled from beneath her huge straw hat and said to Billy in a hushed voice, "She's *adorable*. Just adorable." A man Billy didn't know who was pushing a stroller came toward them.

The man stopped for a second and looked at Sal. He chuckled and moved on. "Never too hot for a fashion plate," he said.

Billy didn't know what that meant. But he *did* know that if you didn't know Sal and weren't used to her, it would be something to see her. She was wearing her tights; red, white, and blue striped shorts; a yellow and pink polka-dot shirt; and her beribboned headband.

Billy just wanted this to be over. He didn't want to run into anyone else. He tried to keep Sal moving as fast as possible. He could feel that his cheeks were hot from embarrassment. They were probably as red as a red permanent marker.

"We'll skip Mr. Tooley's," said Sal. "No mail for dead people."

When they turned the last corner and Billy saw their roof between the trees, he felt lighter somehow. Quickly he pushed the buggy into the garage. And, then, when they were safely inside their own house, his entire body eased up.

"Mama turned on the air-conditioning," said Billy. He could hear the air-conditioner; he could feel the cool air. The beads of sweat on his arms and legs would soon be gone. His sticky shirt would soon be unstuck.

"We're done delivering," said Sal.

"Done forever," said Billy.

"I made lemonade," said Mama. "Come."

The three of them had  lemonade, then settled in the living room with books. Mama and Sal were on the couch. Billy chose the big, soft blue chair.

Billy was surprised that Mama had turned on the air-conditioning. She and Papa tried to use it as little as possible. Papa would say that keeping it off saved money and helped save the world. All Billy knew was that it felt good.

Sal was paging through a picture book with big illustrations of flowers and insects. "'Butterfly, butterfly, Do you know me?'" she said. She'd memorized the book but claimed she could read it.

Billy was reading the graphic novel he'd been given for his birthday. It was called *Commander Seahorse*. It was the first book in a new series. By page three, he'd already laughed out loud, so he knew it was good.

Mama was rereading her favorite book, *Pride and Prejudice.*

"You've read that book a thousand times," said Billy.

"Not a thousand times," said Mama. "But a lot."

"Why?" asked Billy.

Mama shrugged, "I like to read it when I'm happy. I like to read it when I'm sad. When I'm sad, it makes me happy. I guess, I just like to read it."

Billy thought for a moment. "Are you happy or sad?" he asked.

Mama closed her book but kept her finger between the pages to mark her place. "Right now, I'm very happy. I'm with two of my favorite people. And the world feels very calm and hopeful."

Mama sighed. It was contagious, like yawning. Billy sighed and Sal did, too.

Even though Papa wasn't home, Billy felt a closeness, a nearness, to everything. Every thing.

The world *did* feel calm and hopeful.

And then the phone rang.

# 15

Mama picked up the telephone. "Hello?" she said. "What?" She laughed. "You're kidding?"

Billy heard Mama's voice change. "You're *not* kidding?" she said. "Oh no. No. I'll call you back."

Mama hung up the phone. She was blushing. She looked uncomfortable. She went to the front window. She glanced both ways. She shifted her weight from one foot to the other.

"Who was that?" asked Billy.

Mama ignored Billy's question. "Billy," she said, "what was Sal delivering?"

"Mail!" yelled Sal from the couch. "I put *real* mail in the mailboxes."

"Billy?" Mama was looking at Billy with raised eyebrows. She was waiting for an answer.

"I'm not really sure?"

Mama waited for a better answer.

Billy shrugged. "I don't really know, but there was a box of letters or envelopes in the basement. I think Sal maybe, could have, sort of, delivered those . . . I think that's what she did. . . . " His voice trailed off to a thread. He thought to add, "The box was kind of old and smelly."

131

Mama went down to the basement and came back in a few minutes. "Where's the buggy?" she asked.

"I put it in the garage," Billy replied.

Mama went to the garage. When she returned, she said, "No letters." She didn't seem to be talking to anyone in particular, so Billy didn't respond.

Then Mama sat on the couch with Sal and spoke to her in a hushed tone. After that she crossed the room to the stairs and sat on the bottom step. She started taking long, slow even breaths. Billy knew this was not a good sign.

"Can I do something?" asked Billy.

Mama took a very long breath and let it

out before she said, "Yes. You have to go back to every house you went to and get the envelopes. Hopefully most of them are still in the mailboxes."

"Shouldn't Sal do it?" asked Billy. This new development seemed unfair to him.

Mama gave him a look. She also gave him  a paper bag and told him to hurry. "And please, don't read the letters," said Mama. "Just put them in the bag and bring them home."

Billy was glad that Valerie hadn't delivered the mail to this part of her route yet. That meant that Billy didn't have to sort through other envelopes. Another good thing—most of what Sal delivered was still in the mailboxes.

Billy noticed that every piece of mail he collected was either from Mama to Papa or from Papa to Mama. He recognized their handwriting.

Mrs. Metcalf must have seen Billy as he approached her front door. She met him on her porch and handed him three envelopes. "I figured someone would come back for these. So that's what Sal was delivering. She's a little stinker, isn't she?"

At one house, with an empty mailbox, Billy rang the doorbell. A woman he didn't know, but recognized from the neighborhood, answered.

"Did you have some mail in your mailbox?"

Billy asked. He was looking at his sneakers. They were dirty and his shoelaces were frayed.

"I sure did," said the woman.

"Can I have it back, please," said Billy. "It's my mom's." He paused. "It got delivered by mistake."

The woman laughed. She stepped away for a moment and returned with a powder blue envelope with pink lipstick kisses all over it.

Billy opened his bag and the woman dropped it in.

"The regular mail is so boring," she said. "Your mail is much more interesting."

Billy hurried around the rest of the block. He was hot and irritated. When he got home, he went behind the garage and sat in a patch of shade. He looked through the bag of letters. There were hearts on many of the envelopes— Xs and Os, too. Billy knew  without reading the letters that they were love letters.

Love letters! He knew he would never write one. And he knew he would never receive one.

How could Mama and Papa do something so idiotic?

Billy couldn't wait to be done with the letters. He rushed inside.

Mama was in the kitchen standing by the sink. She turned toward Billy when he entered the room. Silently Billy handed her the bag.

"Thank you, Billy," she said. She kissed her finger, then reached out and tapped his head with it. "Thank you, thank you."

"You're welcome," he answered. "There were a couple of houses that didn't have mail and no one answered the door. But I'm not even sure Sal went to *every* house."

"That's fine. It'll work out."

"I didn't read them," said Billy, "but I know what they are." He pitched his voice a certain way to give it the slightest edge. "And now I think I just need to be alone to read my book."

He was mortified to his very core. He hoped Commander Seahorse and the air-conditioning would make him feel better.

# 16

After dinner Mama found a small bundle of letters on the front porch. They were held together with a rubber band. There was a note on the bundle. It said: *Thought you might want these back!* There was a smiley face on the note.

Mama shook her head and put the bundle on top of the bookshelf in the dining room where she'd been keeping the other letters. "I hope it's all of them," she said.

"What do they say?" asked Sal.

"I told you," said Mama. "They're letters that Papa and I wrote to each other before we got married."

"But what do they *say*?" Sal asked again. "Will you read them to me?"

"No," said Mama. She'd said it in such a way that Sal stopped asking questions.

Later Mama's friend, Melanie, came over. She was a history teacher at the same school where Mama taught. Billy heard Melanie talking about the letters. "You'll be joking about it before you know it," said Melanie.

"I doubt it," said Mama.

Melanie laughed. "Anyway, you have more important things to think about."

Billy wondered what that meant.

"Bats, tattoos, now love letters," said Melanie. "You're on a roll."

Billy saw Mama throw up her hands. "I'm ready to be done," she said.

Sal asked if Melanie wanted to play cards.

"Sure," said Melanie.

"War?" asked Sal.

Melanie glanced at Mama with a look of dread.

"How about Crazy Eights?" said Mama.

"War is better," said Sal, "because, if you're lucky, a game could last for hours. Or days."

"Crazy Eights," said Melanie.

So the four of them played Crazy Eights at the kitchen table. Even though it was a game for little kids, Billy had fun. He cared enough to want to win and felt momentarily disappointed if he didn't. He slapped the table and clucked his tongue a few times when things didn't go his way, but he kept his feelings in check for the most part.

Sal did not. She got pouty if she didn't win, and she liked to change the rules to her advantage.

"You two act like there's a million-dollar prize," said Melanie.

"It's not fair," Sal kept whining.

"It's only a game," Mama kept reminding her.

"That's why War is better," said Sal. "It goes so long that sometimes nobody wins."

They took a break for Mama to make popcorn. She even let them put chocolate chips in the popcorn as a special treat. It was a nice way to spend the last night without Papa.

It was late when Melanie left. They all walked her to her car under a glittering ceiling of stars. The air had changed. Before it had been close and still, and now it was clear and light. The wind came and went, came and went, tossing the trees and making the leaves move rhythmically like waves in the ocean.

"Wow," said Mama, "it really cooled off. We can turn off the air-conditioning and open everything up."

"Don't let any bats in," joked Melanie, raising one eyebrow. Papa could also raise one eyebrow. It was something Billy wanted to do, and tried to do, but couldn't.

Mama laughed.

Before she got into her car, Melanie flapped her arms like wings and looked at Sal with a silly expression. Sal screamed. Billy knew Sal was pretending to be scared. But to him, she sounded like a lonely lost animal calling out in the dark.

# 17

Billy woke early in the morning to a loud sound. He'd heard the sound before. It was a siren.

At first he thought the siren was part of a dream. But he was awake and the siren didn't stop. It seemed to get louder and closer.

Before Billy could think what to do, Mama and Sal were beside his bed.

"Don't worry," said Mama. "Let's go. We should go outside. But don't worry. There's nothing to worry about."

"What's happening?" asked Billy.

"A fire truck is coming," said Sal.

"Is our house on fire?" asked Billy.

"Sort of," Mama replied as she hurried Billy and Sal through the house and out to the yard. "But don't worry. It's nothing. It's just the chimney."

Mrs. Metcalf was on the front walk with her dog, Winker. Mrs. Metcalf was looking up.

When Billy looked up, he could see flames coming out of the chimney. The flames, like orange flags, popped out of the chimney and snapped and swayed, then disappeared. Again and again. Thin plumes of black smoke rose up and trailed off, blending into the sky, which was still dim, but starting to lighten.

Everything seemed to be happening at once, and Billy was trying to make sense of it. Mrs. Metcalf was talking to Mama. He heard Mrs. Metcalf say that she'd seen smoke when she was walking Winker; she'd called 911. He heard Mama tell Mrs. Metcalf that she'd had a fire in the fireplace and that she was sure it was just a chimney fire.

Two fire trucks and an ambulance pulled up in front of Billy's house. The fire trucks were enormous and nearly took up the entire block. There were a lot of firefighters in full firefighting gear. Two firefighters talked to Mama. Some went into the house. Others got ladders from one of the trucks and placed them against the house.

More neighbors gathered in the yard and on the street. There was movement and noise all around. The firefighters were in constant motion—on the roof, off the roof, in the house, out of the house. They were like bees buzzing about a hive.

Billy watched intently. How long? It felt like forever—but it also felt like mere minutes of a movie, sped up, made to run faster than normal.

For a moment, Billy had the sensation that the most awful thing was going to happen and that there was absolutely nothing he could do to stop it.

He felt light-headed and dizzy. His mind jumped beyond what was actually happening to a full-blown blaze engulfing the house.

More time passed.

Just when it seemed that all was hopeless, Mama was right next to him (had she always been?) and Sal was, too, and he felt the weight of Mama's hands on his shoulders and he somehow knew that everything would be okay.

"What's happening?" Billy asked.

"Everything's fine," said Mama. Her voice was gentle, but firm, and Billy knew it must be true.

But he still had questions. He looked at Mama expectantly.

"I know this all seems scary," said Mama. "With two fire trucks and the ambulance and the sirens and all the firefighters, but it really wasn't a big deal, and it's over."

"But I didn't see water," said Billy. "They didn't use the big fire hoses."

"They didn't need to," said Mama. "It was a chimney fire, and water would have cracked the chimney. One of the firefighters told me they used dry chemicals. And," Mama added, "when they closed the flue the fire went out. The fire was that small."

"Will it happen again?" asked Billy. "And what made the chimney start on fire in the first place?"

"Something called creosote builds up in

the chimney over time. That's what catches
on fire and burns when there's a fire in the
fireplace. But we'll get the chimney cleaned
and it won't happen again. An easy fix," said
Mama.

Billy glanced around. The flames and
smoke were gone. The firefighters had come
down from the roof. Most of the neighbors
had scattered. The birds were performing

their morning songs. Now the sky was orange
and pink. Billy also realized he still had his
pajamas on. He shuddered.

There was something Billy still didn't understand. He didn't understand why there had been a fire in the fireplace in summer, so early in the morning, to start with. He asked Mama.

"It was my fault," said Mama. "I did something stupid, so stupid."

"You did?" asked Billy. He rarely thought of Mama or Papa doing anything stupid (except for writing love letters).

"I did. I got up early, and because it was so cool outside I decided I'd burn all those letters. So I got a fire going in the fireplace and, one by one, I burned them all." Mama shook her head as if to erase the whole incident. "Bad idea."

Sal, who had been silent for a long time, sprang to life. "You burned the love letters?"

Mama nodded.

"Now I'll never know what they say." Sal seemed genuinely disappointed.

Mama hunched her shoulders. She drew her lips into a tight thin line.

The three of them stood quietly facing the house. Nothing was really different. But everything felt different

Before the firefighters left, one named Tim showed Billy his thermal-imaging camera. "We used it in your attic and throughout your house to make sure there were no hot spots," he explained. "No risk of more fire. You're all safe. And remember—don't ever burn loose paper in your fireplace again," he reminded Mama. "And get your chimney cleaned."

The fire trucks roared away like shiny red dragons.

Now the yard was empty. Mrs. Metcalf and Winker had been the last to go. Billy yawned. Without his knowing it, his fear had turned into something else—a good feeling. He could hardly believe it—two fire trucks and an ambulance had come to his house. His very own house. He didn't think many people could make that claim. He couldn't wait to tell Papa.

And Papa was coming home today! He'd nearly forgotten.

Billy couldn't wait to see Papa. This feeling

overpowered everything else, even his worries. He wasn't worried that anything else exciting would happen. In fact, he'd had so many exciting things happen in the last few days, he thought that maybe he'd had his share and that nothing exciting would ever happen to him again.

# 18

Because they'd gotten up so early, Sal was tired and went back to bed after breakfast. Mama was tired, too; she fell asleep on the couch. And Billy was left alone to wait for Papa.

Billy was making a welcome home sign. He'd found a large piece of poster board in his closet. His original intent was to take his new markers and write "Welcome Home Papa!" As big as possible, with each letter a different color.

After he'd finished the word *Welcome*, he changed his mind. He'd lost his enthusiasm because the sign wasn't looking as professional as he'd hoped. His letters slanted down and got smaller. Also, he was worried that he'd use up his markers. Sal had already used them up enough with her tattoos. And Billy reasoned that if he just drew a quick, simple outline of a house instead of the words *Home* and *Papa*, it would be less wear and tear on his markers and the sign could be reused for other people.

So under the word *Welcome*, Billy drew a house in blue marker because their house was painted blue. He considered adding flames shooting out of the chimney and a bat,

but decided against it. When he was done, he leaned the sign against the wall, then stood back to get a good look at it.

It wasn't nearly as nice as he'd wanted it to be, but he thought Papa would appreciate it anyway.

After that Billy tried to read, but he couldn't concentrate. He had the same problem when he tried to clean his room as a surprise for Mama. He *did* manage to fish out his bat T-shirt from under his bed. It looked like a dusty nest. He wasn't quite ready to wear it again yet, but he rolled it up and stuffed it into his dresser drawer so he wouldn't forget about it.

He wandered around the yard with his soccer ball. It wasn't fun without Papa.

Back inside, Sal and Mama had gotten up and were tidying the kitchen. Billy left them alone and stared out the front window. He noticed that Sal had lined up the Drip Sisters on the windowsill as if they, too, were waiting and watching for Papa.

Mostly he waited on the porch, resting against the big round pillar, his legs drawn up close to his body. Periodically Mama would poke her head out the door and remind him that it would still be a while before Papa got home.

After lunch Mama took Billy and Sal to the library. Billy idled through the rows of books, killing time. Then he sat on a bench by the book return. He closed his eyes and listened when people pushed books through the slot. He heard the books slide for a second, then drop with a nice, solid thump. He liked it when people had a lot of books. Sometimes there was a louder crash. He imagined that a pile of books had formed, then tumbled.

In the nonfiction section, he found a book about fruit bats. He sat on the floor and looked at the photographs in it until Mama said it was time to leave.

Both Mama and Sal checked out about a hundred books. Billy didn't check out any.

"I'm just not in the mood today," Billy explained.

"I understand," said Mama.

But, books or no books, the good thing about the trip to the library was that it had taken up a lot of time, so there was less time to spend waiting for Papa.

As they drove home through the neighborhood, Billy wasn't really thinking anything. The car glided through the curvy streets near his house, in and out of large patches of shade from the thick trees. Billy felt like a twig in a river being pulled along. When they braked for a stop sign, a big black bird on a fire hydrant caught Billy's eye. In the sun, the bird's feathers looked glossy with swirls of color like oil in a puddle.

The bird took off and Billy wished he were the bird. He'd fly so high he'd have a view that would stretch for miles and miles, and he would know exactly how far from home Papa was.

As it turned out, Papa was closer than Billy would have guessed.

Papa was home, waiting on the front porch. He was resting against the big round pillar, his legs drawn up, close to his body. He was sitting in the exact spot Billy had been sitting, in the exact same position.

Mama saw him first. "Look who's home," she said.

"I was waiting right there for *Papa*," said Billy. "And now he's waiting for *me*!"

"No, *me*!" said Sal.

"Me," said Billy.

"Me!" said Sal.

"Us," said Mama.

# 19

Can your heart swoop?

That's what Billy wondered. In the first minutes on the porch with Papa when everyone was hugging and kissing and talking at once, that's what it felt like—it felt like Billy's heart was swooping inside him.

It swooped again when they'd all settled in the living room, and Billy was ready to tell Papa about the fire.

"There's something big we have to tell you," said Billy.

"Big," said Sal.

"Wait," said Papa. "Let me get this straight. There's something bigger than the bat? Bigger than Sal's tattoos?"

"Want to see them?" asked Sal. She didn't wait for an answer. She pulled her tights down so Papa could have a look. Because she was trying to hurry, it was a bit of a struggle. "Almost gone," she said of the permanent marker. She tugged her tights back into place.

"This is *so* much bigger," Billy said loudly, trying to bring everyone's attention back to what was important.

"Mama told me about Sal delivering the mail," said Papa, smiling.

Billy looked at Mama. "After you and Sal went to bed, I talked to Papa," said Mama. "He knows about the letters."

"But he doesn't know about the other part, right?" said Billy.

"Right," said Mama.

"There's more?" said Papa. He widened his eyes. "Did Sal take Valerie's mail truck and drive up and down the block?" He held his hands as if he were gripping a steering wheel and turning it back and forth.

"No!" said Sal. "Papa!" She laughed and couldn't stop as if she'd never heard or seen anything funnier.

Billy couldn't wait any longer. "We had a fire," he blurted out. "Mama burned the letters and the chimney started on fire and Mrs. Metcalf called nine-one-one and *two* fire trucks and an ambulance came and there were tons of firefighters and they went on the roof and all through the house." Billy stopped to take a breath. Now his heart was really swooping.

"Whoa," said Papa. "Slow down."

All the while Billy was talking, Mama was smiling and nodding and moving her hands as if to say: *But everything's fine.* And then she *did* say it: "But everything's fine."

"No one got hurt?" asked Papa.

"No one got hurt," said Mama. She

explained everything that had happened more clearly than Billy had and with more details.

"Wow," said Papa, shaking his head. "I missed all the excitement."

"Papa?" said Sal. "What did the letters say? Mama won't tell me."

Papa burst out laughing. "I don't really remember," he said. He pulled on his beard and raked his fingers through it. "I guess we could write new ones," he joked. He raised one eyebrow and wriggled it.

"No," said Billy.

"What will they say?" asked Sal. "Will they be about kisses?"

"Yes," said Papa. "Big, fat, wet, sloppy kisses."

Sal squealed with delight.

Billy groaned.

Mama just smiled. Then she put her hands on her stomach and said, "Welcome home."

Upon hearing Mama's comment, Billy jumped up. "Papa, I made something for you. I almost forgot." He bolted from the room.

When he returned, in a flash, he was proudly holding up his welcome home sign for Papa.

"I love it," said Papa. "Did you use your new markers?"

Billy nodded. "And I drew a house instead of writing the words *home* and *Papa*, so that we can reuse the sign."

"Smart move," said Papa.

Sal looked at the sign and she looked at

Billy. She ran to her room and came back with a little lion eraser with a missing tail.

"Welcome home, Papa," said Sal handing over the lion. "You can keep him. I don't really use him anymore."

Billy rolled his eyes.

"Thank you," said Papa. "Thank you both. You're shredding my heart." He put the sign from Billy on the mantel and he placed the little lion in front of it. "Nice," he said admiring his gifts. "Maybe I should go away more often."

"No," said Billy.

"No," said Sal.

"We still need to hear about art camp," said Mama.

"Why don't we go to Ruby's Cupboard for dinner," said Papa, "and I'll tell you all about it?"

"Yes!" said Billy, pumping his fist. Ruby's Cupboard was his favorite restaurant. It served the best onion rings he'd ever had.

"Yay!" said Sal. She danced in a circle around Papa, flapping her bent arms like a chicken.

Billy and Sal were ready—buckled into the car—before Mama and Papa had even left the house.

This was the kind of excitement Billy liked—everyone was home, and he was going to have onion rings the size of doughnuts.

# 20

Under the twinkling lights and the brightly colored lanterns at Ruby's Cupboard, Mama, Papa, Billy, and Sal had what Billy would call a feast, which included some of his favorite foods: onion rings, fried cheese curds, and chocolate milkshakes.

While they ate, Papa told them all about art camp. "I learned so many new things. I learned about welding and glassblowing and I spent a lot of time using a potter's wheel trying to make a vase."

"Did you bring the vase home?" asked Mama.

"I wasn't very good at using the wheel. But I did keep a few of my sorry attempts. I'll show you after dinner."

"But you're good at everything," said Billy.

"I'm not," said Papa. "But thank you for the compliment." He winked at Billy.

"What was your favorite thing?" asked Billy.

Papa took a moment to consider this. He studied the onion ring in his hand as if it held the answer. "I think I would say glassblowing. I have some things to give you."

"What?" asked Sal.

"You'll see," said Papa. "At home."

They were too full to each have a dessert, so Mama ordered one hot fudge sundae with four spoons.

On the drive home, Billy wondered if he'd ever eat again.

"Everyone, meet in the kitchen," said Papa as they were getting out of the car.

Mama, Billy, and Sal went to the kitchen, and Papa disappeared somewhere. He entered the room carrying a covered wooden box.

"What's inside?" asked Sal.

"Orbs," said Papa. "I'm calling them orbs."

"What's an orb?" asked Billy.

"Something round," said Papa. "A ball. A sphere." He paused. "The sun, the moon, the planets—they're orbs."

Papa set the box on the table and removed the lid. Inside were five glass orbs. They were

mostly clear, with swirls of color. They looked to Billy like giant marbles.

"I made them," said Papa.

"They're beautiful," said Mama. She picked one up and turned it in her hand. "They *are* like little planets."

"I like this one," said Sal, touching one with ribbons of red running through it.

"I like *this* one," said Billy, nudging a

different one with his finger. It was blue and green like the Earth.

"There's one for each of us," said Papa.

"But there are five," said Billy. "And just four of us."

Sal pointed and counted, starting with herself. "One, two, three, four," she said. "Mama's a teacher, but you're not," she said to Papa. "Maybe you're not a good counter."

"Papa can count," said Billy.

Billy looked at Papa. Papa was looking at Mama.

Billy looked at Mama. Mama was looking at Papa.

They looked and looked and looked at each other.

Then Mama nodded.

"You say it," said Papa.

"No, you," said Mama.

"What?" said Billy.

"What?" said Sal.

"Let's say it together," said Papa.

Papa whispered something to Mama. Then he said, "One, two, three—"

Then, together, Mama and Papa said, "We're having a baby!"

"A real one?" asked Sal.

Mama and Papa laughed.

"Yes, a real one," said Mama.

Billy could hardly believe it. A baby! For just a moment, the air seemed charged. Billy was quiet, taking it all in. He realized with a rising giddiness that life was going to change; everything was going to be different.

"When?" asked Billy.

"December," said Mama.

"Will it be a boy or a girl?" asked Sal.

"We don't know," said Mama.

"It'll be a surprise," said Papa.

"Girl," said Sal. "I think it's a girl."

"That's why I've been so sleepy lately," Mama explained. "And I think that's why I overreacted about the letters."

"I knew it!" said Sal.

"You did not," said Billy.

"Maybe I did," said Sal.

And then, suddenly, something dawned on Billy. "Oh," he whispered. He paused, thinking about it. "Come with me," he said urgently. "Everyone, come with me."

Billy led everyone to the living room, to the fireplace. "Look," he said, pointing to the mantel. "Look at my welcome home sign. Maybe I didn't put Papa's name on it for a reason. Maybe I knew there was going to be a baby. Maybe I knew there was going to be someone else to welcome home."

"Amazing," said Mama.

"Remarkable," said Papa.

Billy felt so happy, he had to wiggle his toes and blink his eyes, and if he'd wanted to stop smiling, he wouldn't have been able to.

He had made a wish on his birthday—and then he'd spent every day regretting it. Now he wouldn't change it for anything.

He'd wished that something exciting would happen. And his wish was coming true. It was coming true in the best possible way.

Have you read
*The Year of Billy Miller?*

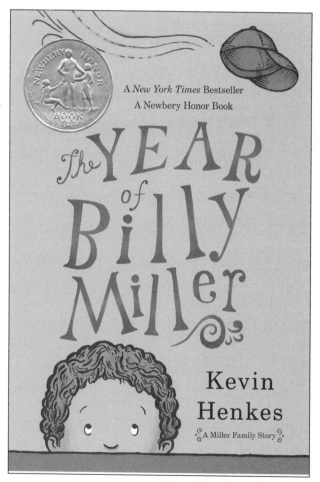

It was the first day of second grade and Billy Miller was worried. He was worried that he wouldn't be smart enough for school this year.

There was a reason he was worried. Two weeks earlier on their drive home from visiting Mount Rushmore and the Black Hills of South Dakota, Billy Miller and his family stopped in Blue Earth, Minnesota, to see the statue of the Jolly Green Giant. Billy instantly recognized the Giant from the labels of canned and frozen vegetables. The statue was spectacular—so tall, and the greenest green Billy had ever seen.

Billy was wearing his new baseball cap that said BLACK HILLS in glossy silver embroidery. It was a blustery day. The flag on the nearby pole snapped in the wind. Billy raced ahead of his family—up the steps to the lookout platform. As he stood between the Giant's enormous feet, a sudden gust lifted his cap from his head. His cap sailed away. Without thinking, Billy stepped onto the middle rung of the guardrail, leaned over, and reached as far as he could. He fell to the pavement below.

The next thing Billy remembered was waking up in a hospital. His parents, whom he called Mama and Papa, were with him, as was his three-year-old sister, Sally, whom everyone called Sal.

After tests were done, the doctor proclaimed Billy miraculously unharmed, except for a lump on his head. "You fell exactly the right way to protect yourself," the doctor told him. "You're a lucky young man."

"And Papa got your hat back!" said Sal.

When they returned home, Billy proudly showed his lump—and his cap—to his best friend, Ned. He called his grandmother on the phone and told her about the incident, too. Everything seemed all right until a few nights later when Billy overheard his parents talking in the kitchen.

"I'm worried about him," said Mama.

"He's fine," said Papa. "Everyone said he's fine. And he seems fine. He *is* fine."

"You're probably right," said Mama. "But I worry that down the line something will show up. He'll start forgetting things."

"He already forgets things," said Papa. "He's a seven-year-old boy."

"You know what I mean," said Mama. She paused. "Or he'll be confused at school. Or . . ."

That's all Billy heard. He snuck up to his room and closed the door. And that's when he started to worry.

# Read all about the Miller family!

★ "The moments that appear in these stories are clarifying bits of the universal larger puzzle of growing up, changing, and understanding the world."

—*Kirkus Reviews* (STARRED REVIEW)